Dear Parent:

Congratulations! Your child is taking the first steps on an exciting journey. The destination? Independent reading!

STEP INTO READING® will help your child get there. The program offers books at five levels that accompany children from their first attempts at reading to reading success. Each step includes fun stories, fiction and nonfiction, and colorful art. There are also Step into Reading Sticker Books, Step into Reading Math Readers, Step into Reading Write-In Readers, Step into Reading Phonics Readers, and Step into Reading Phonics First Steps! Boxed Sets—a complete literacy program with something to interest every child.

Learning to Read, Step by Step!

Ready to Read Preschool–Kindergarten
• big type and easy words • rhyme and rhythm • picture clues
For children who know the alphabet and are eager to begin reading.

Reading with Help Preschool–Grade 1
• basic vocabulary • short sentences • simple stories
For children who recognize familiar words and sound out new words with help.

Reading on Your Own Grades 1–3
• engaging characters • easy-to-follow plots • popular topics
For children who are ready to read on their own.

Reading Paragraphs Grades 2–3
• challenging vocabulary • short paragraphs • exciting stories
For newly independent readers who read simple sentences with confidence.

Ready for Chapters Grades 2–4
• chapters • longer paragraphs • full-color art
For children who want to take the plunge into chapter books but still like colorful pictures.

STEP INTO READING® is designed to give every child a successful reading experience. The grade levels are only guides. Children can progress through the steps at their own speed, developing confidence in their reading, no matter what their grade.

Remember, a lifetime love of reading starts with a single step!

STEP INTO READING®

Featuring characters from your favorite **DISNEP** and **DISNEP·PIXAR** movies!

Tales of Fun & Friendship

Step 1 and Step 2 Books

A Collection of Six Early Readers

Random House 🏠 New York

Contents

Disney · PIXAR

TOY STORY 2

Me Too, Woody!

by Heidi Kilgras

illustrated by Atelier Philippe Harchy

Random House 🏠 New York

Buzz and Woody.

Good buddies!

Game time.

Checkers!

"Me too, Woody!"

"No, only two."

Buzz and Woody.

Good buddies!

Playtime.

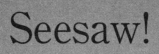

Seesaw!

"Me too, Woody!"

"No, only two."

Poor Jessie!

"Hey, Jessie."

"Want to play?"

"Yay!"

Play ball!

Big swing.

Big hit!

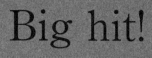

"Run, Buzz!"

"Run, Jessie!"

Going.

Going.

Got it!

Good play!
Good buddies!

DISNEY · PIXAR

FINDING NEMO

Just Keep Swimming

by Melissa Lagonegro

illustrated by Atelier Philippe Harchy

Random House 🏠 New York

Nemo has a dream.
He wants to join
the school swim team.

But Nemo has
a little fin.

He thinks that
he will never win.

Dory helps Nemo.

She teaches him
to go, go, go!

Nemo races and races.

Nemo chases and chases.

"Just keep swimming,"
Dory sings.

But Nemo thinks
of other things.

"I will never win.

I have a bad fin."

"Just keep swimming!"
Dory cries.

So Nemo tries . . .

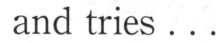

and tries . . .

. . . and tries.

Nemo races and races.

Nemo chases and chases.

Yippee! Yahoo!

His dream comes true.

Nemo makes the team.

Can Nemo win the
first-place prize?

"Just keep swimming!"
Dory cries.

Watch him race.

Watch him chase.

Watch as Nemo wins
first place!

STEP INTO READING®

STEP 2

DISNEY's
Lilo & Stitch

Go, Stitch, Go!

by Monica Kulling
illustrated by Denise Shimabukuro and
the Disney Storybook Artists
designed by Disney's Global Design Group

Random House 🏠 New York

Lilo waved to Myrtle.

She wanted to be

Myrtle's friend.

"I got a new dog!"

Lilo yelled.

"His name is Stitch."

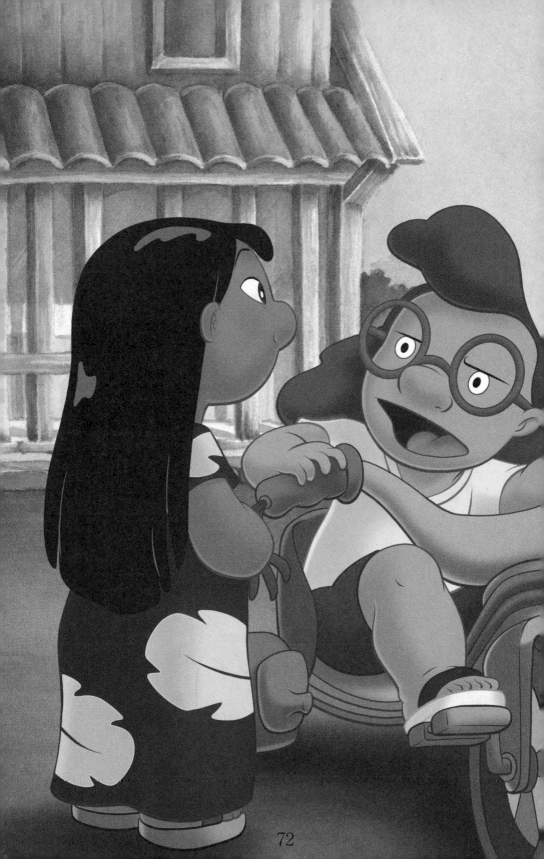

Myrtle rode up
on her new trike.
"Wow!" said Myrtle.
"That dog is ugly."
Stitch made a face.

Stitch was <u>not</u> a dog.

He was blue and furry.

He had big ears.

And he had sharp teeth.

Stitch was really

an alien!

Pleakley and Jumba

were aliens, too.

They had come to Earth
to catch Stitch.
Pleakley tripped over
Jumba's foot.
"Whoa!" said Pleakley.

Stitch saw Pleakley.

Then he saw Jumba.

He had to get away!

Stitch had an idea.

He grabbed
Myrtle's trike.
He grabbed Lilo's hand.
They took off!
Stitch rode fast!

"Hey!" yelled Myrtle.

"Oh, no!" said Pleakley.
"Stitch is getting away!"

"Grab that scooter!"
said Jumba.
"We will catch him!"

Lilo and Stitch rode
under a waterfall.
Splash!

They got all wet.

But Lilo did not care.

"Cool!" she cried.

Jumba and Pleakley

rode under

the waterfall.

They got soaked.

They did not like it
one bit!

Stitch came to a cliff.
There was nowhere to go.
Just lots and lots
of water.

Stitch turned right.

Lilo hung on tight.

Jumba and Pleakley
zoomed right into
the water!
Lucky for them,
someone was surfing!

Lilo and Stitch
zoomed right
through a market!
"Yum!" said Lilo.

"Ooof!" said Pleakley.
Jumba drove into
a bunch of bananas!

Stitch rode past
a volcano.

It began to rumble.

Smoke and

lava came out.

"Uh-oh!" said Lilo.

"Go, Stitch, go!"

Stitch rode faster.

"We have him now,"
said Jumba.
The aliens
were getting closer.

But so was
the lava!

Jumba and Pleakley
jumped off the scooter.
They climbed a tree.

And Lilo and Stitch
got away!

"That sure was fun!"
said Lilo.
"Let's do it again!"

DISNEY'S
THE WILD

THE KOALA KING

by Apple Jordan
illustrated by the Disney Storybook Artists

Random House 🏠 New York

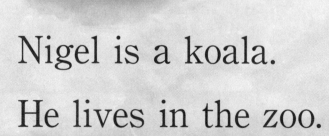

Nigel is a koala.

He lives in the zoo.

Toy koalas are cuddly.

But Nigel is not a toy.

He does not like
being cuddly.

He wants to be
big and strong.

Samson is a lion.

He _is_ big and strong.

He tells his son, Ryan,

about the Wild.

One day,

Ryan was taken

to the Wild.

Samson had to get
Ryan back.

Nigel and his friends
wanted to go, too.
Samson told them
it would not be safe.
But they had to help.

The gang set sail
for the Wild.
They had to find Ryan.

The trip was
long and hard.
Nigel was hot.
Nigel was hungry.

Nigel was fed up.

He jumped

off the boat.

Nigel hit land.
They reached
the Wild at last!

The gang went
in search of Ryan.

But Nigel fell behind.

He was on his own.

Nigel met a pack
of beasts
in the Wild.

They bowed
down to him.
They were happy
to see him.

Long ago
a toy koala
had fallen
from the sky.

The toy saved the beasts
from hungry lions.
It was a sign
that one day
the beasts would rule.

Now a real koala
had come to the beasts.
The beasts thought
Nigel would help
them rule the Wild.

They made him
their king.
Nigel liked being king.

The beasts found some
of Nigel's friends.
They even found Ryan!

But the beasts wanted
to cook his friends.
Nigel had to think fast.

Samson showed up
just in time!
Nigel needed help.
They made a plan
to save the gang.

Nigel tricked
the beasts.
He faked a fight
with Samson.

It worked!
The gang got away.
They even made
some new friends.
Nigel saved the day!

The friends headed
home at last.

Nigel threw
the cuddly toy away
once and for all.
He proved that he was
one big strong koala.

The Sky Is Falling!

by Apple Jordan

illustrated by the Disney Storybook Artists

designed by Disney Publishing's Global Design Group

Random House 🏠 New York

Chicken Little
made a big mistake.
He rang the town bell
to warn everyone
that the sky
was falling.

But the sky never fell.
His dad, Buck, said
it was only an acorn.

Everyone teased
Chicken Little.
No one would let him
forget his mistake.

Chicken Little was tired
of being teased.
He wanted
things to change.
"Today is a new day,"
he said.

135

Chicken Little joined
the baseball team.
"Maybe my luck
will change,"
he thought.

His luck did change!

He hit a home run.

He won the big game!

Chicken Little

was happy.

His dad was proud.

Things were better.

But then
there was trouble.
The sky really did fall
on Chicken Little!
A piece landed
right in his bedroom.

Fish, Abby, and Runt
came to help him.
Fish picked up
the piece of sky.
It floated in the air.
It flew out the window.
Fish flew out with it!

The friends raced
to help Fish.
They saw a spaceship
in the sky.

The friends snuck
onto the spaceship.
Fish was there!
And they learned that
Earth was in danger.
They had to tell
someone!

Chicken Little ran
to the school.
He rang the bell.
Ding! Dong!
"Aliens!" he cried.
"Aliens are here!"

Everyone thought
Chicken Little
was crazy.
Even his dad.

But soon Buck

saw it for himself.

The sky was

falling apart!

Chicken Little saw
an alien kid running.
He knew he was lost.

He had to return

the alien kid

to his parents.

Buck and Chicken Little
faced the aliens.

The Earth was not
in danger after all.
The aliens were only
looking for their child.

Chicken Little
gave the alien kid
back to his family.

Now the aliens
could go home.
Chicken Little
was a hero!

Things had changed after all!

Disney · PIXAR
Cars

Driving Buddies

adapted by Apple Jordan

illustrated by the Disney Storybook Artists

Inspired by the art and character designs created by Pixar Animation Studios

Random House 🏠 New York

McQueen was
a race car.

He was shiny and fast.

He wanted one thing—
to win the big race!

Mater was a tow truck.
He was old and rusty.
He wanted one thing—
a best friend.

Mater lived
in a little town.
The streets were quiet.
All was calm.

One night,
McQueen got lost
on his way
to the big race.

He sped into
the little town.
Sheriff chased him.
McQueen got scared!

He flew into fences!

He crashed into cones!

He ripped up the road!

He made a big mess.

McQueen was
sent to jail.
He met Mater there.
Mater liked
McQueen right away.

Sally, the town lawyer,
and the other cars
wanted McQueen
to fix the road.

McQueen could not
leave town until
the job was done.

McQueen got to work.

He was unhappy.

Mater wanted

to show him some fun.

He took McQueen

tractor tipping.

It <u>was</u> fun.

McQueen told Mater
why he wanted
to win the big race.

He would have fame
and a new look.
He would be a winner!

Mater was happy.

He had

a new best friend.

McQueen fixed

the road at last!

The news reporters

found McQueen!

Mack the truck
was glad to see him!
It was time to go
to the big race.

Mater was sad
to see his buddy leave.
The other cars
were sad, too.

So Mater and his friends
went to the racetrack.
They helped McQueen.

But McQueen still
did not win.
He helped an old friend
finish the race instead.

Now he knew
that winning was not
what he wanted most.

What he wanted most
were friends.

If you know the alphabet and are ready to read, look for these Step into Reading books:

✿   A Barbie Reader
✪   A Disney Reader
♦   A Phonics Reader

➤   A Thomas the Tank Engine Reader
✎   A Write-In Reader

STEP INTO READING®

If you can recognize familiar words and sound out new words with help, look for these Step into Reading books:

ALL STUCK UP
BARBIE: A DAY AT THE FAIR ✿
BARBIE: LOST AND FOUND ✿
BARBIE: ON THE ROAD ✿ ✎
BARBIE: TWO PRINCESSES ✿
BEARS ARE CURIOUS
BEAR'S BIG IDEAS ✎
BEEF STEW
THE BERENSTAIN BEARS
   BY THE SEA
THE BERENSTAIN BEARS
   CATCH THE BUS
BEST DAD IN THE SEA ✪
BONES
BUZZ'S BACKPACK ADVENTURE ✪
CAT AT BAT
CAT ON THE MAT
COUNTING SHEEP ✦
DAVID AND THE GIANT
DINOSAUR BABIES
A DOLLAR FOR PENNY ✦
A DREAM FOR A PRINCESS ✪
FIVE SILLY FISHERMEN ✦
GO, STITCH, GO! ✪
HAPPY BIRTHDAY, THOMAS! ➤
HENRY'S BAD DAY ➤
HERE COMES SILENT E! ◆
HOME, STINKY HOME ✪
HONEYBEES
I LOVE YOU, MAMA ✪
IS IT HANUKKAH YET?
JAMES GOES BUZZ, BUZZ ➤
LITTLE CRITTER SLEEPS OVER
MICE ARE NICE
MOUSE MAKES MAGIC ◆

MY LOOSE TOOTH
MY NEW BOY
NO MAIL FOR MITCHELL
OH MY, PUMPKIN PIE!
ONE HUNDRED SHOES ✦
PEANUT
A PET FOR A PRINCESS ✪
PINOCCHIO'S NOSE GROWS ✪
P. J. FUNNYBUNNY CAMPS OUT
P. J. FUNNYBUNNY'S BAG OF TRICKS
PLATYPUS!
A PONY FOR A PRINCESS ✪
POOH'S EASTER EGG HUNT ✪
POOH'S HALLOWEEN PUMPKIN ✪
POOH'S HONEY TREE ✪
POOH'S VALENTINE ✪
QUICK, QUACK, QUICK!
READY? SET. RAYMOND!
RICHARD SCARRY'S PIE RATS AHOY!
RICHARD SCARRY'S
   THE WORST HELPER EVER
SEALED WITH A KISS ✪
SILLY SARA ◆
SIR SMALL AND THE DRAGONFLY
SIR SMALL AND THE SEA MONSTER
THE STATUE OF LIBERTY
SURPRISE FOR A PRINCESS ✪
THE TEENY TINY WOMAN
THOMAS AND THE SCHOOL TRIP ➤
TIGER IS A SCAREDY CAT
TOAD ON THE ROAD
TWO FINE LADIES: TEA FOR THREE
WAKE UP, SUN!
WHISKERS
WHOSE FEET?

✿ A Barbie Reader
✪ A Disney Reader
✦ A Math Reader

◆ A Phonics Reader
➤ A Thomas the Tank Engine Reader
✎ A Write-In Reader